# A Diary of Joseph...

*-a spiritual journey through time-*

## DIANE PROCTOR REEDER

Published by Written Images, Inc.
(248) 356-8310

Book Design by Danielle Funderburg
Art by Leah Reeder and David Reeder

Scripture quotations marked (NIV) in this book are from the HOLY BIBLE,
NEW INTERNATIONAL VERSION (NIV). Copyright © 1973, 1978, 1984
International Bible Society. Used by permission of Zondervan Bible Publishers.

Scripture quotations marked (NLT) are taken from the Holy Bible, New Living
Translation, copyright © 1996. Used by permission of Tyndale House
Publishers, Inc., Wheaton Illinois 60189. All rights reserved.

Scripture quotations marked (KJV) are from the King James Version of
the Bible.

ISBN 0-9705721-0-7


Printed in the United States of America
1     3     5     7     9     10     8     6     4     2

# Dedication

*for Terry*
*who told me*
*to write*
*and taught me to push*
*all the way through*

*It was not in vain*

# Contents

# Preface

"How's the book coming?" said my friend Mary innocently. She was the one who read the draft with a critical eye, and her feedback both encouraged and frightened me.

She told me that she sensed I was holding something back. I knew she was right, because I am a private person. I was hoping that I could keep this a self-explanatory allegory and not explain much about its origins.

This book was to be an allegory of suffering and victory, a comparison between the sufferings of the biblical Joseph, who spent years as a falsely accused prisoner, and my family (natural *and* spiritual), who spent years caring for our husband/father/son/son-in-law/brother/brother-in-law, and yes, friend, Terry.

Joseph's ending was truly remarkable. He moved from chief prisoner to Pharaoh's viceroy in the twinkling of an eye. When my husband Terry became ill with leukemia, I thought that his (our) end would be similar.

I was wrong. We humans often are. But I continued with the writing of this book, and continued to keep out our personal story as much as possible.

Mary saw it differently. She challenged me with these words:

"Plunge into the deep."

She had no idea what she was telling me.

A few months before my husband Terry died, I wrote these words as part of the Preface:

> Later, as Terry began to recover, only to relapse and endure the horror of a bone marrow transplant, I was given more and more to say about this Joseph story that I felt we were re-living. I was given other poems too, poems that have sustained me through years of hard yet strangely wondrous waiting. And I have found that the waiting has produced a growing peace and an incredible confidence in God's ability to make us whole, and then heal us.
>
> I will not tell you any more details, except to say that Terry is alive and healing. And so am I.
>
> I am glad that it is God's hand covering our lives, and not the hand of another.
>
> Our prayer is that anyone who has suffered—not just from illness, but from anything—would find perspective and strength to continue on their own spiritual journey.

After he died, I thought the book was in vain. Everything was hollow, as it so often is after such a loss. But I have come to believe (even though I don't yet fully understand) that these words are still true. Terry is alive and healing. And so am I.

# Introduction

Every book has a story. Every author has a different vision, a different reason for putting words to paper. This book is no different.

The story of this book starts in 1987, when Terry and I were expecting our first child. I was given a name for a book, a name which I tried to change as the idea evolved, but to no avail. The title was the same as you see on the cover: *A Diary of Joseph.*

The idea of the book was this: When we read the Scriptures, we are not always given information on what these men and women of God thought and felt. The Joseph story in Genesis takes up several chapters and gives a lot of information (Genesis 37:1–50:26). However, we get very little of the process Joseph had to go through in order to be transformed from a spoiled and favorite son to the top regent and administrator in Pharaoh's vast kingdom.

Back to 1987. As I wondered about Joseph and what his spiritual journey might have been like, I was given three lines of a poem to be used in the book:

> *I gave my heart to bitterness*
> *I regurgitated strange waters*
> *My bowels and eyes burnt with anger*

That was it. Nothing else came. I read books about people who had been falsely accused and imprisoned to get a feel for their experience. I thought about what form the book might take. But nothing else came.

I pushed the book to the back of my agenda. We had another child, my husband Terry and I were both working, and I semi-forgot about the book. After all, what had I suffered?

The concept of the book never went away, even during this time. Its title held on and held on in the back of my mind, and stayed there until the Lord knew it was time for me to understand.

I'll never forget the day. Terry had gone to emergency a few days before with a lump on his neck, and they admitted him. Admitted him! Someone whose doctor less than a year earlier had declared him "healthy as a horse."

I went to see him at the hospital on the way to running an errand. He seemed to be doing well, and I was confident that the doctors would give him some pills and send him back home to us.

I walked into the room and heard the words no wife ever wants to hear.

"I have leukemia."

Leukemia? All I knew about it at the time was that Ali McGraw died from it in *Love Story*. We both cried for a few minutes, but I was just stunned. And all but numb.

I had yet to make the connection.

After that was a whirlwind of tests, hospital pamphlets, and doctors' assurances that leukemia was highly treatable and even curable. Plus, in his case, it had been caught early—another good sign.

So off we went, into a chemotherapy-filled fog, not knowing the impact that that poison would have on our lives. . .

One day—in fact, two days before his last round of chemo, Terry had a major allergic, potentially fatal response to an injection dye that the doctors had ordered for a routine test. Just a few hours later, he became confused and his speech was nearly unintelligible. He was in intensive care for a few days and ended up with infections in virtually every organ of his body. He lost the use of his legs and went from working 70 hours a week into a place of utter dependency—on doctors, nurses, and especially on family. For a while—about six weeks—my mother-in-law and I, and my father- and sister-in-law on the weekends—took shifts so that we could watch him around the clock. We knew that the medical staff simply could not keep such a close eye on him, and we were afraid for his life.

After what seemed an interminable wait to see if the chemo had worked, we found that it had. But not before taking its toll. And not before I knew without a doubt what experience would allow me to write this book.

More than half of this book was written during that period, in a hospital room in the middle of the night, watching my husband suffer and flail away at a demon of sickness that hit him so hard and so fast he had no time to even prepare. What was given to me was given at a point of desperation—both mine and his. I was being given words almost faster than I could write them, and I have remained faithful to those original words.

Three months after Terry was diagnosed, he went into a rehab facility, in remission. He went in on a stretcher, and came home three weeks later on a cane—something he told everyone within earshot he would do!

A couple of weeks after coming home, he had ditched the cane and was walking with me to our son's T-ball games. We had a lot of fun that summer. We had no idea what was coming.

What came was a bone marrow transplant that was itself miraculous: his sister Leah was what they called "a perfect match." Then nearly three years of cancer-free living that came with too many medical complications to even list here. Months of relative health, then problems that took him, all of us, back down to places of desperation we never imagined we'd reach.

Then relapse in January of 1998.

He'd had so many miraculous recoveries, we thought that this was just another test of our faith. It was.

On Sunday, June 28, 1998, Terry died. He fell on the floor from his bed, and I went to him, frantic. He nodded to me a couple of times, and I tried to pick him up, called my neighbors, called emergency, and felt his pulse ebb away from me. I never dreamed this would happen. I had it all figured out—or so I thought.

The closer we get to the Author and Finisher of our faith, the more we come to understand the vastness of His mystery, and the magnitude of the work He is doing in the universe—and in our lives. We will never have it all figured out.

"For my ways are not your ways," says the Lord in Isaiah 53. God's glory is all tied up in His mystery.

One of my favorite quotes is from an author who I now consider a friend:

Madeleine L'Engle, who reviewed one of my earliest manuscripts and wrote a personal note of encouragement. In her book *Many Waters*, a fictionalized account of Noah and his family before the flood, she put in one of the angel's mouths these words:

"Goodness does not guarantee safety."

When I read that, a wonderful peace came over me. For if I have no guarantees, I can stop grasping at them, and instead hold on to Christ my Rock as He takes me through Many Waters.

And so we begin. . .

4/16/94

*Dear Terry,*

*You know what? You asked me today (or maybe it was yesterday), "Are you keeping a diary?" And I said yes, which was kind of true. Three entries in six weeks. Not much, but I've been kind of tired lately, and drained, you know?*

*I got another epiphany today, but I have to give you some background first. You know I've talked to you about my book, "A Diary of Joseph?" The thing that I kept thinking to myself was, "You will never write that book unless you have a time of suffering." And I wondered what I would possibly have to go through in order to write about a man who went to jail for God's glory.*

*So this is it. Sickness is like jail. You're trapped, you wonder when it will end and how much more you can take.*

*Oh Lord, I said. This is the kind of suffering you chose for us. I always thought I was set apart for something significant, and always wanted to be used of God.*

*This wasn't quite the kind of suffering I had in mind. In fact, I didn't have anything in mind. I frankly hoped I could skip right over it to the book.*

*But then what kind of book would it be?*

*Terry, you and I are supposed to write this book together. And Leah is supposed to illustrate it. I truly believe that. If I tell you that tomorrow, will you promise to hurry and get better?*

*I love you.*
*Diane*

*To every thing there is a season, and a time to every purpose under heaven: A time to be born, and a time to die; a time to plant, and a time to pluck up that which is planted; A time to kill, and a time to heal; a time to break down, and a time to build up; A time to weep, and a time to laugh; A time to mourn, and a time to dance; A time to cast away stones, and a time to gather stones together; a time to embrace, and a time to refrain from embracing; A time to get, and a time to lose; a time to keep, and a time to cast away; A time to rend, and a time to sew; a time to keep silence, and a time to speak; A time to love, and a time to hate; a time of war, and a time of peace.*

*Ecclesiastes 3:1-8*

*… He hath made everything beautiful in His time…*

*Ecclesiastes 3:11*

# CHAPTER ONE

*Innocence & Wonder*

# INNOCENCE & WONDER

*Then God remembered Rachel; he listened to her and opened her womb. She became pregnant and gave birth to a son and said, "God has taken away my disgrace." She named him Joseph.*

### JOSEPH: "INCREASER"

#### *Joseph Is My Name*

My Name is Joseph.
My father Jacob is the grandson of
one whom God chose to sire a nation.
We are a proud family,
my brothers and I.

My mother Rachel is beautiful.
I think my father loves her best.
It shows in the way he treats me.
I get the most attention,
the best clothes,
the least chores.
I am his favored one.
I love my father.

We are a proud family.
My father says that we will start a nation.
I do not know exactly what that means.
But I want to be a part of it.
After all, my name means "increaser."
I want to do great things.


### The Beginning

*I am going to do a great thing in your life,
but first I will have to plant you.*

Plant me?

*Yes. And it will be very deep in the ground. You will know
when it happens. You will be in a place of unknowing, a
place of testing.*

What will I not know?

*If you knew that, your faith would not sustain you. True
faith requires a level of not knowing of a type that I cannot
describe. When it happens, you will know it, as I said.*

### *Joseph at 17*

I was tending the flock with my brothers
Really they are just half-brothers
not of my mother Rachel
but of the slave-wives

Father,
Dan, Naphtali, Gad, and Asher
have not done according to your instructions
what will you do with them?

### *Jacob's Lament and Joy*

My mother had a favorite—me.
My father had a favorite—Esau.
I used that to my advantage
and stepped into the status of my brother Esau, the first-born. . .

But I was repaid.
God got me back.
He let me be tricked into
marrying the wrong woman.
It was too late.
But my whole being was love
for Rachel,
and I learned to wait.
Leah bore to me first,

but I waited for Rachel.
And then Joseph came.
Joseph, the first son of my life's love.

The joy of his birth overwhelmed us;
everything was sharper, clearer, more beautiful.
He was perfect, and so
I bought him
a coat.


### *Joseph had a dream...*

Am I the center of the universe?
I dreamed that I was.
Or at least, I was the center of attention.
The first dream
was about my produce and my brothers' produce
(Theirs bowed down to mine).
The second dream
was about the whole realm of nature (It bowed to ME).
Did God make me higher than the galaxies?
What does that mean?
What will become of it?
What position will I have?
Will it really happen?

*Yes. I have confirmed this twice to you, and my words*
*will try you and refine you many times over.*

My dream was not quite as ambitious as Joseph's. It was this book. But I had the same kinds of questions. Why does the idea keep coming back? Why doesn't it fade from my interest and memory, as so many others have? How will this all come together? Is this my life's vocation? Will it really happen?

Like Joseph, we would be tried again and again before the word spoken came to pass.

CHAPTER TWO

The Pit

# THE PIT

*His brothers said to him, "Do you intend to reign over us? Will you actually rule us?" And they hated him all the more because of his dream and what he had said.*

*Genesis 37:8*

The first pit is a place of excitement and anticipation. It is also a place of fear. But the adrenaline from all the emotions kind of runs together, and you have a lot of energy—and optimism.

But first, you have to get over the shock…

*Those who go down to the pit cannot hope for Thy faithfulness.*

*-Isaiah 38:18b*

### *An Explanation*
He dreamed God's dreams
but with a fatal flaw
He had to <u>know</u>
Like Adam/Eve,
he wanted to eat
from the Knowledge Tree
the Tree of Separation

of the distraction
of righteousness that is by the law
and not the grace

as he ate
of its truth
only part real
he slowly made his way
up the mountain, then
down
to the pit.


**A TIME TO HATE...**

### *Brothers' Lament*

Who does our brother think he is,
taking the lion's share of our father's love?
If only he were not here, we. . .

Never mind.  He is here.
Our hate outweighs our father's love.

Let us be rid of him.
Let him suffer as we have,
older yet debased in our father's eyes.

What's the best way to suffer?
We could kill him.


**Reuben**

But death is the end of suffering.
Will his death make Father love us more?
I think not.
Let us make him brood here
in the pit for a while.
Let him think about
his arrogant ways.
Let us make his agony long and full.
How can he dream from there?


**Judab**

He is not my full brother; what does it matter?
After all, I am born of the first wife
I should be the favored one.

A few shekels of silver
should soothe my father's heart
It certainly will mine.

After all, I am born of the first wife.

Solomon was right. There really is a time to mourn. I began mourning the day I found out Terry had leukemia. Sometimes I felt God's strong presence in the most tangible ways. Sometimes I was dry as dust. Sometimes I was surprised in the midst of mourning by inexplicable, wondrous joy.

I wonder if Reuben's mourning deepened his faith or made him think about the course of his life. Because, isn't that really the point?

I thank God for my times of mourning. Especially when they turn into dancing.*

Because, isn't that really the point?

*Psalm 30:11*

### A TIME TO MOURN...

#### *The Earth Melts*
*thoughts from Reuben*

When sin happens
it is particular
not general,
individual

Tree leaves droop
just a bit;
blades of grass
huddle together
afraid of what is to come;

the earth's core widens
to melt just a little
more crust
remembering the everlasting fires
that punish and purify.

If i am in tune,
i draw in my breath
my heart skips a beat
and i suffer in the particular,
groaning with creation.*

Sometimes it is alright
to be depressed.

*Romans 8:22*

### *The Thing That Cannot Happen*

I watch my brothers leave me in the pit,
My mouth agape in horror.
Then they come back.
I knew they couldn't leave me here long.

Wait!
What's this?
They're selling me like a piece of meat!
The way Uncle Esau sold his birthright to my father

Will I ever see my family again?
My mother Rachel?
My father Jacob?

This is worse than death
I thought I would be a ruler; now I am a slave
sold to the descendants
of Hagar, a slave-wife

I am falling, suffocating under the weight of
my own dreams
They are too heavy
for me to carry

Or perhaps
I did not
carry them well.

How did they allow this to happen?
How did God?

**A TIME TO GIVE UP AS LOST...**

### *Jacob*

My sons approach
No... No... No...
Joseph's coat of all colors
splattered with blood
Surely the blood is his

Killed by a beast
How could God allow this?

I am repaid twice for my ways
of trickery and deception
Rachel, and now Joseph
Detestable      detestable
I cannot bear this unspeakable thing.

Jacob gave Joseph up as dead. But he wasn't dead; he was just lost. I do not believe in "giving up as lost" anything the Lord gives you—until He, with finality, takes it away. And even then, you must know that He is able to redeem.

### *Forsaken*

Fingers feel the muscles on my legs
poke at my ribs
pry open my eyes and mouth
their fingers are rough
my skin too yielding

My shame is now complete
I live the life of
a slave
lower even than my half-brothers
born to the slave-wives
Lower than the wives themselves

My head is bowed
I am far, far away
from the realm of nature bowing to me

My dreams are cast off
into outer darkness,
forgotten . . .
Their death is hard and sure.

Why have you forsaken me?
Father, you did not prepare me for this.

CHAPTER THREE

Reprieve

# REPRIEVE

*For Joseph was penetrated by the certainty that he had not been
snatched away to no purpose, that rather the planning intelligence
which had rent him away from the old and led him into the new had
plans for him in one or another way; and to kick against the pricks, to
shrink from the affliction, would have been a great sin and error—
these being one and the same in Joseph's eyes.*

*"For all the manifold shapes of things were first present in the thoughts
of God, and the work, borne by the breath of God, is
their begetter."*

*"Potiphar was silent. . . He felt a warmth in his face, his breast, and
all his limbs, a sort of dim stirring: it held him to the spot and would
not let him go.*

Thomas Mann. *Joseph in Egypt.* NY: Alfred A. Knopf,
a division of Random House, Inc., 1938.

As the wife of a leukemia patient, I now can begin to understand the agony
of waiting in the dark...

I dreamed that I was rowing a boat, trying to get to a certain island. But the
shores beckoned. I began to move slowly sideways, until I got so close I
decided to get out and take a rest. It felt good. I thought I was safe. Then a
beautiful creature appeared. The sun came out. All was well.

That was short, I thought. Maybe I don't have to row that far after all. This was easier than I expected. (Like me, before the second bone marrow biopsy. Like Joseph, when the baker was let out of jail).

Just as suddenly, the beautiful creature metamorphosed into a horrible, grasping evil. Darkness fell, and I felt its hands on me.

I had let my guard down. I didn't want to do the work to get to the shore.

There must have been a turning point with Joseph, where he recognized what God wanted to teach him. What did he recognize? When did the light come on?

### ...A Time for Peace...

#### *Does Goodness Guarantee Safety?*

I am a servant in a rich household.
If I act very good, maybe
God will let me go home.
I will do everything right—
I will leave nothing undone—
and God will bless me.
I am not abandoned forever.
I am part of a greater plan.

## JOSEPH AND POTIPHAR

Potiphar—
*your speech*
*is not like a slave*
*your wisdom*
*is not consistent with your station*

Joseph—
*I was born to a shepherd*
*who owned much land*

*He wrestled with God-Most-High*
*built altars*
*and bowed low*

*I have seen many things*
*but only one impresses me:*
*The hand of God in my life.*

Potiphar—
*Joseph, I will make you chief steward*
*shepherder of all that I have*
*I will not withhold anything*
*from you.*

Remission from cancer is like a reprieve. Initially, you're on edge, because you don't know the length of the relief. But then you settle into old routines, and it almost feels like normal.

But not quite. It's hard not to wonder if (when?) the other shoe will drop.

Potiphar's Wife—
   *This Joseph*
      *is an attractive boy*

   *He must miss home*
      *Did he love someone there?*

   *She is not here;*
      *But I am.*

   *Joseph!*
   *Joseph!*
   *Joseph!*
   *Lie with me!*

   *Servant, I command you—*
      *Come here!*

### *Making Arrangements*

This woman, Lord.
She approaches me.

*I see.  Your strength has kept you clear of her advances.*

Does that mean I get to go back home?

*That is not the point.*

I am starting not to like it here.

*That is not the point either.*

What is the point?

*The woman is my servant.  She answers to me.*

You are making her do these things?

*I don't make anybody do anything.  I observe, and arrange, and influence.*

And you are arranging this for me?

*I am arranging **you**.*

## A Time To Shun Embracing...

### *Why Joseph Ran*

I remembered:
my father at the brook
Uncle Esau's forgiveness
My mother's love

The ravaging of my sister Dinah—
the horror and death it caused

Pictures from God Himself,
coming back to remind me of what I must know:
His faithfulness
His call to obedience.

Potiphar's wife repels me.

## A Time to Tear Down... A Time To Keep Silent...

Potiphar's Wife—
*Servants!*
*See what Potiphar has done to us!*

*Bringing in this despised, haughty Hebrew*
*putting one of such lowly stature*
*in charge of you all.*

*And now he has shamed me*
  *skulking around me when none of you was here to protect*

*Joseph*
  *will never see the light of day*
  *I will see to it.*

*See what Potiphar has done to us!*


Potiphar—
  *Something about this man*
    *constrains me*

  *I do not trust my wife*

  *She is very beautiful*
    *But I have been this way before*

  *I see the way she looks at him*

  *I cannot let this go...*
    *I must take action*

  *This poor man is a mystery to me*
    *He is of great integrity*
    *Oppressed and afflicted*
    *Yet he does not open his mouth*
    *As a sheep before her shearers is silent*

*According to the law, he is worthy only of death*
*But how can I unbalance the scales?*
*This man I have come to trust with my own life?*

*My wife is an embarrassment to me*


Mrs. Potiphar—
*Joseph, answer me!*
*I can speak life or death.*

*Joseph, don't you hear me?*
*Insolent slave,*
*how dare you remain silent!*

# CHAPTER FOUR

*The Bottom*

# THE BOTTOM

**LAMENTATIONS:**

> *He has led me into darkness*
> *a valley no light can reach*
> *nothing to illumine the smallest*
> *step I take.*

David Rosenberg. *A Poet's Bible.* NY: Hyperion, 1991.

Every hospital stay seemed to be another bottom. Terry went back in for a bone marrow transplant in 1995. It went well at first, and then many, many complications. Many times of hearing, "I don't know that he'll ever fully recover," and "He may not make it through the night." But we had been through so much in 1994, that nothing seemed as bad to us as it looked to the doctors.

The bottom is where you do a lot of waiting. You must find ways to occupy that time. If you don't, you'll come out the same person—and what is the point of that?

### *...and Counting*
*Joseph.*

Yes, Lord?

*Can you wait?*

Wait for what?

*Can you wait?*

How long?

*It doesn't matter. Can you wait?*

What do I do while I'm waiting?

*You change. You rest.*

Change into what? Rest how?

*You start to look like me. You rest from your striving against yourself. And Me.*

I don't understand.

*You will. Joseph?*

Yes, Lord?

*Can . . . you . . . wait?*

Yes, Lord.

*So will I.*

### Letting Go

I'm losing myself.

*That can happen.*

My foundations are cracking.

*You were on the wrong foundation.*

How can I fix it?

*You don't. You change it.*

How?

*You can only rest on my word, for my word is Myself. Put nothing else there but that, and then let me build your life.*

*After all, I have ordained this foundation before the collective memory of all your ancestors.*

*The earth can melt and the moon turn to blood,*
*But My foundation cannot be shaken.*

### *Pressing & Promise*

You're pressing me.

*"Pressed down, shaken together, running over..."*

What?

*Never mind. That comes later.*

My head hurts.

*Sometimes you think too much.*

I'm always wondering about my dreams.

*Like I said. Sometimes...*

Will the heavenly bodies really bow to me?

*Don't try to figure it out.*
*Just let the dream unfold.*
*It will.*
*I promise.*

When you suffer, every day is a challenge. Your thoughts run rampant and roughshod over your emotions. Your spirit and soul exhaust themselves in worry and futility. I am sure that Joseph, being human, must have experienced this range, as he imagined (dreamed?), questioned, and argued with the only One he knew could give the answer.

**A TIME TO SPEAK...**

I'm in a fighting mood today, Lord. I need to ask you some questions.

*Like what?*

Do you expect me to be here, in this place, forever?

*There are some things that I cannot let you see right now.*

But I must know. Now.

*No, you don't. Now is what you must know.*

What can you tell me about my future?

*I can tell you that it will be*
*the sum of your sins,*
*the sum of your virtues,*
*the sum of all your experiences, your thoughts—*

*and my sovereign will.*

I don't understand that.

*It's past human understanding. Your language is not full enough to grasp or define it. The real understanding can only come from My Spirit.*

———

When you are in a place of pain, and you know God, He gives you guideposts—beacons of hope. With Noah, it was the olive branch that the dove brought back. With Jacob–Israel, it was the time of wrestling with the angel.

For us, it was Terry's statement at the beginning: "The Lord told me this was not unto death." We held, clung to, rehearsed that line in our hearts over and over again.

What was it with Joseph? Perhaps it was when he was able to interpret the dreams, and the cupbearer promised to remember him to the king.

But plans sometimes go awry. Remember? The cupbearer forgot his promise, and went on his merry way.

*Maybe he had others. For such a long stay, he would have had to.*

**JOSEPH**

I cling to all pieces of hope. Today, I saw a small beetle whose foot brushed a spider's web. The bottom part of its fragmented body was beginning to become entangled. But it fought—I've never seen anything like it. I could almost see him thinking.

He fought hard, but he just got more entangled. So he rested. Then he gently pulled and turned—just enough to pry the bottom of his body loose from the sticky new threads of the web.

He sat there looking at it, for a while, almost as if to celebrate his victory. Then he crawled down the walls and slipped under the door to freedom.

### *Clarification*

Lord, don't you want me to be happy?

*No—I want you to learn to be content.*

But that seems so... boring.

*Oh, no. You have the wrong idea. Contentment accumulates with experience touched by trouble. It signifies strength that is deep in your spirit.*

## Not everything that occurs to our minds is of God...

It is hard not to lapse into mindless daydreaming. When I see other families, it's especially hard. I close my eyes and imagine what it would be like to go back. Then, I get frustrated.

Relief that comes from unrealistic daydreaming is illusory, transient. I needed something permanent. Living in the present is a lot more comforting if you're not making up stories.

### *Vain Imaginations*
I'm pretending.

*Pretending what, Joseph?*

Pretending I have my life back.

*You have your life.*

This is not my life. I will not accept that.

*You must not let circumstances drive you. You must do the life you are given. This is the life that, right now, you have been given.*
*It is still a gift.*
*What will you do with it?*

### *Invitation*

*Go deeper.*

What, Lord?

*Go deeper.*

I don't understand.

*I know. But you will. I know what you will find.*

Is it me?

*It will always be you. And Me.*


### *Unknowing. Mystery. Beyond.*

I am utterly in the dark.

*But I know what is in the darkness.*

What is there? I must know.

*Riches. Treasure. Occasions for stumbling. Despair. But you must choose.*

How can I choose?

*You choose according to what your ancestors taught. I will walk with you through the hard choices, even if they are wrong. I will whisper in your ear, turn this way, then that. But first you must believe that I will give answers to those that seek.*

*Just remember: I AM.*

### Time. Time. Time.

When, Lord?

*It is not time yet, Joseph.*

But I've been praying and praying.

*I know. It takes time for me to answer prayer.*

But you are God. You blessed my father after just one night with the angel.

*How many years had your father sojourned on this earth before that happened?*

*(Joseph is silent.)*

*It took time to build the pyramids. It takes time to cross a desert. It takes time for a baby to be born.*

*How much more time, then, to build a life?*

*"Everybody's life is more difficult than you think."*

-*Lucille Clifton*
From *The Language of Life: A Festival of Poets.* Bill Moyers, ed.
NY: Doubleday, 1995.

### Envy

I wish I were back with my brothers.
They have the land, freedom, father, life.

*You don't know what they have.*
*How do you think they face your father every day*
  *knowing what they have done?*
*The furtive fugitives, sneaking at living*
*Watching words*
*Seeing their father die daily.*

*What kind of life is that?*

Chemotherapy affects nearly every part of your body. It is brutal and unforgiving. When it started affecting Terry, those first three lines of a poem I had written seven years before, but could never complete, came back to me like a flood.

I saw him "regurgitate strange waters." I saw even his bowels and his eyes ravaged by the poison of chemo. I saw his mind and spirit repulsed by what was happening to his body, and his powerlessness to stop it.

It is easy to become bitter when you feel you are getting what you do not deserve. I think that all of us have tasted that bitter water.

But that is not the whole story.

I also saw him roar back like a threatened lion. I saw him tell everyone within earshot that he was not always going to be this way. That his legs and arms and fingers and speech would be restored.

Much of what he said came to pass—in ways that delighted some of us, and shocked others.

How shocked Joseph's old Egyptian cellmates and keepers must have been when he finally was released from prison. And Mrs. Potiphar must have been struck dumb.

### *Relentless*

I gave my heart to bitterness
I regurgitated strange waters.
My bowels and eyes burnt with anger.
My pupils' briny water were my only drink.
In one day, I lost everything.
Hope became cynical—a bitter laugh, a wounded cry.

What is happening?
This is not the life
I envisioned.

But now, I can no longer see.
I am groping and wallowing in the darkness.
Who is there for me?
God has abandoned me
again.

*The valley wherein you sit*
*is a door*
*that will allow you and your people*
*to escape from this place*
*and live at the level*
*of hope.*

*Death is in my mind today.*
*Like the longing of a man for his home.*
*When he has passed long years in captivity.*

From *When Egypt Ruled the East,* by George Steindorff & Keith Seele.
Chicago: Univ. of Chicago Press, 1963

*To conquer the beast, we must first make it beautiful.*

*-Ancient Chinese proverb*

*Vex not thy spirit at the course of things, and heed not thy vexations. How*
*outlandish. . . it is to be astounded at anything that happens to you in life.*

*-Marcus Aurelius*

The Lord never ceases to surprise. In the midst of agonizing suffering, He will visit, just to give some relief, some sense of His presence. He did that with us many times over. And it came at the most unexpected times.

### *Waiting for Hope*

When you wait
 in the abyss

like Jesus
 in the garden

like Jacob
 with the angel

like Shadrach
 in the flame

like Mary
 at the cross

You are at the apex of your strength.


### *Waiting... Again*

Lord?

*Yes?*

The plan with the cupbearer didn't work out.

*Yet.*

So I'm back to waiting again.

*Do you know what you're waiting for?*

I'm waiting for hope to come.

*You are, right now, at the apex of your strength.*

### Unexpected

I feel light today, Lord

*That's because I'm carrying you.*

I thought you always carried me.

*I do. It's just that sometimes I have to lift you up from the ground. The pull that holds you to the ground can make you feel heavy sometimes. That's when I lift you up.*

Sometimes hope is what keeps you alive. Just make sure you are hoping for the right thing.*

*Galatians 5:5

CHAPTER FIVE

Hope

# HOPE

## I KNOW WHAT THE CAGED BIRD FEELS, ALAS!

*I know what the caged bird feels, alas!*
*When the sun is bright on the upland slopes;*
*When the wind stirs soft through the springing grass,*
*And the river flows like a stream of glass;*
*When the first bird sings and the first bud opes,*
*And the faint perfume from its chalice steals —*
*I know what the caged bird feels!*

*I know why the caged bird beats his wing*
*Till its blood is red on the cruel bars;*
*For he must fly back to his perch and cling*
*When he fain would be on the bough a-swing;*
*And a pain still throbs in the old, old scars*
*And they pulse again with a keener sting —*
*I know why he beats his wing!*

*I know why the caged bird sings, ah me,*
*When his wing is bruised and his bosom sore, —*
*When he beats his bars and he would be free;*
*It is not a carol of joy or glee,*
*But a prayer that he sends from his heart's deep core,*
*But a plea, that upward to Heaven he flings —*
*I know why the caged bird sings!*

*by Paul Lawrence Dunbar*

### Goals

You must get to the place
where worry
        becomes request

anger
        turns into action

fear
        gives way to fervor

despair
        hopes in the dark

Still yourself there

then walk

toward the light.


### Dreaming... Again

I had a dream. I was lying on my back, looking at the ceiling.
The ceiling's been closing in on me lately. But last night, I
started sweating. And the sweat was as big as drops of blood.

*That was your living water.*

What is living water?

*It is the product of the Spirit.*
*It is Light*
*It is Center.*
*It is sufficient.*
*It is like unto the Son of God.*

What does it do?

*It draws you to Me.*
*It invites you to drink*
*and be satisfied*
*with enough.*

### Forever

My hope is not a line
        but a circle
It begins at a point
        before time
        and stretches around
        past time
        into eternity
that doesn't "continue"
but just *is*.

June 14, 1994—

Terry is getting better. We don't know it, but in two weeks he'll be out of the hospital and on the way to rehab. Sometimes the time just before deliverance is the hardest time. You're out of the crisis, the place where your whole mind is centered on survival. But you know you're not out of the woods yet. So how do you keep faith? When the adrenaline of crisis drains away, how do you keep walking a straight path?

### *Relentless (of a different sort)*

*Keep knocking.*

But my knuckles hurt.

*Keep knocking.*

But I'm tired. Why do I have to beg you over and over for the same thing?

*You are not a dog that you should beg. You are my child. Keep knocking.*

What's the point?

*There is learning in every knock.*

How can I learn just repeating myself?

*After you knock, you have to listen.*

Listen for what?

*A quiet voice that brings wisdom and answers.*
*But only if you...*

I know. Keep knocking.

I think I know why God glories in mystery. It's a partnership, really - He glories in mystery, and we glory in the search.

Sometimes, though, I think we do best to let the mystery lay, and just marvel in it.

### Unready
*I have given you vision.*

But every time I get it into focus, it dies.

*You've not yet really had it in focus.*

Is that why you keep taking it away?

*You're not ready to receive the glory of the vision I have for*
*you. But when you are, you will become a large tree, in*
*whose branches many birds will nest and find refuge.*

## A TIME TO SEARCH . . .

### *Remembering*

Lord?

*Yes.*

What was it like for my father when my mother died?

*It was bitter, dry like a desert, acutely and achingly painful.*

What did he do? How did he handle it? I must know.

*He mourned—You must have a mourning period. He marked his place of mourning. Then he moved on.*

Is it time for me to move on?

*Not yet. You're not out of your period of dryness. Soon, you will be saturated like the morning's dewey grass. Soon, you will have fatness, good oil and bread. But it is not time.*

Somehow, that does not satisfy.

### *Asking*

El
continue to draw me to
        Yourself
that I may eat

        drink

           and play

in Your joyous waters
        and so
gain sustenance
        to work
while it is yet
Day.

Joseph must have moved from 'denial' to faith – I think we all do.
The first stage is denial that something so horrible could happen. You're not worried, not because you have faith, but because the prospect of failure is too devastating to imagine. But denial does not plant the seed. Faith plants it. Consistency and praise water it. God wants to bring us to the point where we will not be moved by any person or circumstance, but only by Him.

"Diane, I had the most incredible dream," Terry said to me one night. When I asked what it was, he told me: "My grandfather came to me."

Terry's maternal grandfather, Major Holley, died in 1969. But his words were clear and lucid and sure. He wasn't hallucinating. Nothing was wrong with his brain. When he told me, he was at peace-and in awe.

"What did he say to you?" I knew not to question.

"He just waved his hand and said, 'Go on. Go on.'"

From what he had told me about his grandfather, who the grandkids affectionately called "Tunta," it sounded like him.

The Bible says we have a cloud of witnesses. Hebrews 11, one of the great "Hall of Fame" chapters of people of faith, mentions saints like Abraham, Noah, Rahab.

God doesn't mention Tunta-he hadn't been born yet. But in that dream, for Terry – and for me – Tunta joins that great cloud. Witnesses who cheer us from the sidelines on the other side, and tell us: "Go on. Go on."

**A SPECIAL VISIT**

> ***abraham         isaac         jacob         joseph***
> My great grandfather Abraham came to me last night.
>
> *What did he say?*
>
> He said, It is almost time for you to break forth.  What does that mean?
>
> *You come here new, hoping, eager.*
> *Your leaves shoot new growth.*
>
> *But the growth is wild.*
>
> *It must be cut back before it consumes and devours.*
>
> *Sometimes the cut is swift and sharp.*
> *Sometimes a lingering.*
> *But the cut must come.*
>
> *Then, you break forth again.*
>
> *This time the shoots are an*
> > *ordered wildness*
> > *charcoal holy*
> > *fiercely glowing*
> > *meek*
> > *directed*
> > *into the path of glory.*

I have been cut to the quick; is it almost my time?

*It is.*

How will I know?

*You will know.*


### Testify
*Did you know you were helping me write your story?*

No. Who is putting the words down?

*I AM. On your heart. I write My ways into your heart, and you help Me to finish the story. Didn't you know that your life is a story that will be read?*

Who will read it?

*The people around you now. People from your past. And people you cannot even imagine.*

How?

*Look around you. The vastness of the night sky—do you remember? Everyone into whom I breathe the breath of life is written on a scroll—their thoughts, motivations, actions, tears, joys—*

And we'll get to read them one day?

*—and one day it will all be revealed. Shouted from the housetops, a cloud of witnesses, testifying of heaven.*

Joseph was chastened at the pit to impart humility, blessed with Potiphar to bring hope, scourged in prison to learn dependence. Then, and only then could he be trusted to handle victory.

### *The End of the Beginning*
I plant myself. Right here. I am not moving.

*But don't you want to get out of this place?*

Yes. But I'm setting my stake here, and I purpose to trust you. I almost feel like a tree.

*Planted by the rivers?*

. . . of water
I shall not be moved.
Even if you keep me here until I die.
I shall resist bitterness.
I shall resist pitying.

I shall resist my own blindness, my own groping. . .
I shall resist myself, my own weaknesses, my own fears.
I shall fall upon your grace and mercy.

### *A Learned Contentment*

My heart magnifies you today
I will build my temple here
right here
put my altar in it
and take both where you may lead me

*That is the place. That is the place I want you to be. Now,
you are truly free.
I know.*

*Resistance is the secret to joy.*

From *Possessing the Secret of Joy,* by Alice Walker.
Publisher: Harcourt Brace Jovanovich, 1992.

# CHAPTER SIX

*A Strained freedom*

# A Strained Freedom

What is it like to get out of prison? Do you automatically shout for joy, or is the moment more sober? God has not designed our emotions to change so readily. You might certainly be happy that you are "free," but there is a period of disorientation. To protect yourself, you put a lid on your emotions. Then you wonder why you're not as happy as people tell you you must be (or worse, "should" be).

This very dryness, which happened to me when Terry came out of the hospital the first time, helped put me on a level place. It was a place of quietness and reflection, albeit frustrating. When you don't have a lot of water, you put your energy into conserving instead of trying to grow new leaves and flowers—which can be exhausting. It was really a part of my healing, along with Terry's.

But trust me—joy did come later. Like a flood. And interestingly, it didn't stop any of us from making more mistakes. Like Joseph.

**A Time to Heal...**

> Lord, you've changed my circumstances,
> but I feel dry. Dusty.
> That is the way I choose to be.
> I was tired of going up and down like an old leaf
> with every wind of change.
> When I am dry, I don't have to feel.

Being dry protects me from heights
                giddy but dizzying
and from depths
                raw and despairing.

*One day, you will learn to appreciate*
*the pure joy of the heights*
                *without dizziness*
*and the purposes I have in the depths*
                *without despairing.*
*But stay here awhile.*
*There is much learning to be had in the dryness of the soul.*
*Remember—*
*Blessed are the poor in spirit.*

The time after the first hospital stay was harder than I thought it would be for us. In the hospital, everything I had to do was given. I had to be there. I had to talk with doctors. I had to work, to see to our children.

Terry, too had to do things. His life was even more circumscribed than mine.

In a way, it made things so much clearer for me. I didn't have to figure out what to do. I already knew. The priorities were clear.

I don't think it was so easy for Terry. Mostly, he was simply miserable to be where he was. His circumscribed time was laced through with frustration and fear and such a loss of independence and dignity.

So when he got home, we did some flailing. We had to adjust to a new kind of "normalcy." Neither of us really knew how to do that.

At the same time of this disorientation, we were absolutely ecstatic for him to be home. We felt everything at the same time. And underlying was the knowledge that the process may not be over yet.

Everything came at us so fast. A couple of weeks after he was home, I had to take our son, David, to a baseball game. Terry urged me to go without him. Of course, I didn't want to. What if he died while I was gone? What if he fell? I stood there and cried for a minute. Then I left with David.

When we got back, all was well. I was calm again. I learned that his healing was the real thing; I wasn't sure at first. I certainly didn't want to go back to the former place, where everything was defined. But we were really confused about how to live here, in such an unfamiliar place. We even had to do some fighting, some steam-blowing, to get to the next level.

Yet another level of living—of healing.

It all came so fast.

### *Is This All There Is?*

Once days were stagnant
Sitting waters
Or droning and relentless
like a continual dripping

Now, time moves too fast
I blink and everything is new
It is joyous to me
everyday pleasures
small but luminous
and I want to hold it all to myself
hold the world
close to my breast
clamp down hard
so it ceases to spin

I don't know where to turn
what to do

My movements were once defined for me
now, I must carefully select
choosing among many things
instead of just a few

That, too, is its own prison.

### *Zaph'nath-paaneah*

*Saviour of the World*

And Pharaoh said:
Who else is like Joseph?
Surely the Spirit of God rests with him.
Joseph, no one is as wise as you.
Come, rule over my house;
all will do whatever you say.
Your word will be my law.

Watch, as Joseph rides in the chariot.
Watch, as his handlers cry:
Bow the knee! Bow the knee!

Watch, as Pharaoh says:
No man will lift so much as a hand or a foot
without the word of Joseph.
I will change your name to Zaph'nath-paaneah,
for you have saved our world.

Watch, as the beginnings of a dream unfold.

Pharaoh re-named Joseph Zaph'nath-paaneah, which means "Savior of the world." In our society, we have tragically forgotten the power of the name. It can define us and help us to remember. In the ancient days, primitive peoples took great stock in the naming of a person. Sometimes God gave the parents what to name the child, as in the case of John the Baptist. Sometimes the parents took the name from the circumstances surrounding the birth, as Sarah did when she named her son Laughter (Isaac), because it tickled her so when the Lord told her that her old and wizened womb would bear a child.

Did God give Pharaoh what to re-name Joseph? Was Joseph, for the Egyptians, a forerunner of Christ? What did Joseph teach them? Did they learn the lesson that God intended?

### Baby Steps

I am feeling my way
in an unfamiliar place
with bumps and craters
in unexpected locations

The glory
must go before me
if only to light my feet
I don't ask for much

*The ocean*
*and the heavens*
*display only my handiwork*
*you cannot get your arms around me*

*so gird up*
*unclench yourself*
*open wide*
*all that you are*
*and let Me go beyond*
*the feet*
*as I flood your small world*
*with light*

*Only then will you find*
*that you are not*
*in a tunnel*
*but in open air*
*where you can walk*
*then run*
*then fly*

*Breathe deeply*
*Expand your vision of me*
*and grow into blessing.*

### *Beauty for Ashes*
The woman, Lord.

*Asenath?*

Yes. She is beautiful. But she does not worship as I do.

*Her beauty replaces the ashes of your former life.*

How do I do this? How do I live with so different a person, a woman outside my tribe, unfamiliar with our ways?

*With gratefulness. Her name means "dedicated to the god Neit". Now, she will be dedicated to you. That is all the explanation I will give now. You will have to wait to see what is to come.*

You have always made me wait.

*Every year, you wait for the harvest. This is the same.*

I am given to understand dreams, debased, sold into slavery, freed in the twinkling of an eye—and then you give me a foreign wife. Unusual things are happening.

*I AM an unusual God.*

### The Challenge of the Blessing (Feeding the Multitudes)

I am pressed on every side
by people who don't think I'm doing this right
the grain bins are too small or too large
"How are we going to feed all these outsiders
            and our country too?
"The lines are too long."

Some would have my head.
They see me as an interloper
("Who is this man?
A Hebrew, an adulterous prisoner?
Who does he think he is?")

They would that I had never lived.

I am pressed on every side
But this is familiar to me
My body was pressed into the pit
My mind was pressed by Potiphar's wife
My spirit was pressed within the dungeon

I know this pressing
I can wear lightly the garment
for it is light and momentary,
leading into grace.
I am protected by——pressed into——the Secret Place.

What is it like to live fully in the Spirit? I am afraid that few of us really know.
I am afraid that most of the time I do not know.

But I do know that if we walk the same paths we did before our trial, we're
not walking in the Spirit. We wish that it could be as it was, when things

were easier and we didn't have so much to think about. We often try to get back to that place, even as God is trying to push us into another.

As for us, much of the thinking was about healing. I was just starting to look into alternative treatments, but that was a scary world for me. We had people praying, we called for the elders to lay hands more than once, and we saw even in the doctors and the medicines the hand of God.

But was it enough? We never really knew.

True faith is sometimes a plunge. It can be so scary. Once you jump, it is exhilarating. But it comes with such a great responsibility.

And for us, the matter was life and death.

Our old life was so much more comfortable. I missed it terribly.

### *Wistful*

Something is breaking in me
          and I am sad
          an odd sadness
          at once light and heavy
          gaining and losing.

I want to cling to the old comfort
          rather than embrace
          the new wildness

the awesome freedom
the terrible responsibility
of life lived
truly
in the Spirit.


### *Almost There*

I am on the verge
 of a clapping
 a dancing
 a joy
 a laugh
but I am afraid
of the next step.
 is it the abyss?
 or the large free place?
will the joy crush?
the laughter stop?
the heart melt?
how do you live
 here

   now

     unafraid

fully aware
of God's blessing
in *this* place?

### *Mourning Into Dancing*
The chastening of the Lord
(afflicting for the moment)
persuades me to turn
provoking lushness of
fruit and flower

A garden enters my soul
raising my hands to receive His grace
and I am renewed like the eagle

I walk in another space today
It is a place of healing
where balm is continually applied
where I continually receive it
to keep bitter roots from springing
and I am being made whole

*Is there no balm in Gilead? Is there no physician there?*

—*Jeremiah 8:22*

Yes, there is a balm in Gilead. Look at Joseph. Look at Mary Jesus's mother. Look at Jesus. Look at me.

I found out that there is a balm in Gilead. As I read through the Word, the balm literally jumped off the pages, and God applied them directly to my wounds. I could only look up in awe.

As I continued writing the words of this book, trying to faithfully put down what I was given, I experienced God's healing. You must do what God has given you to do. Otherwise, the healing will never fully come. What a sad thing, to walk through life limping; not because you wrestled with the angel, as Jacob did, but because you did not listen for—and to—His voice.

### *Asenath*

Zaph'nath-paaneah,
You who have colored my life
with insight
and the wind of the Spirit
I have given you a son.

You are such a strange man to me.
Strange and familiar, all at the same time.
You worship another God, and call Him by name.
Can I know this God?
Will you let me call Him by name?
Pharaoh has told us to do according to your word.

Our son will be called Manasseh
With him,
the past is memory
and you can live in the now.

I am come to love you,
whose father named you Increaser,
and whose Pharaoh named you Savior-of-the-World.
I have come to love you, Joseph.


### Joseph's Response

God has given me this lovely woman
and I fall into her arms, weeping
She is soft and gentle.
She loves me—I don't know how.
We are so different.

I tell her of my family,
and how we lived by the seasons, just as they do (but with less
fanfare).
Springtime, harvest, moons, stars, cycles.
And I tell her of our God, El.
Whom we cannot see,
Whom we cannot build or make,
yet He speaks to us.

His speech is loving and intimate, I tell her.
Even when He brings trouble,
He provides comfort.

Just as you have provided me, I tell her.

God has given me water
and grain
and progeny
in the desert of my affliction

the spring rises up
and takes away my dryness

The pit—
the narrow place
through which I passed—
has given birth
to the new Joseph.

With Manasseh's birth Joseph said he had forgotten his father's household.
Of course, he hadn't.

### *Looking Back*

It is time to move on
and forget my painful past .
the scourge of the pit . . .
the naked examinations of slavery . . .
the rage of hateful brothers who betrayed me . . .
the seductress

who took her shame
out on me . . .
the jail where my freedom
extended only as far as the walls
and almost made me forget my dreams.

Bless God, who has given me Manasseh
to help me forget.

I only wish my father were with me.

**A Time to Sew Together...**

### *Joseph's Lament*

I have been given the object of my longing:
Freedom.

In some ways, slavery was better
I had no choice
and every excuse.

Sometimes I prefer the clay feet of prison
where I could not fly
to the wings of freedom
where I must.

Now that I must perform
responsibility is relentless, pounding, insistent;
I suffocate.
In some ways, I want to go back
but I would not.

Much awaits.

*To whom much is given, much is required.*


### It is Finished
You have put me in a wide place
my feet on solid ground
my sky the limitless eternity.

*You have not finished the test.*

CHAPTER SEVEN

The Last Test

# THE LAST TEST

The memory of my brothers
stains my conscience
not enough to block my view
just enough to color
the way I look at the world.

It is clear that Joseph is angry with his brothers when he first encounters them as an adult. I've read the arguments that he was simply trying to test their character, but the Scripture text simply does not bear that out. Joseph is mad!

With his new power, Joseph tries to wreak out some semblance of revenge, but in the end finds he cannot. He thinks his brothers are the problem. But when he sends them home, without Benjamin, God begins to work on him once more. What kind of encounter must that have been! We can only imagine how much spiritual work it took to unravel the hard knot in his soul.

I'm sure that it was this wrenching encounter with God that exploded him into love—love for his brothers who so shamefully wronged him, and love for his God who so faithfully pruned him.

"You meant it for evil," he told them. His love wasn't just sentiment. The years hadn't clouded his memory. He knew fully, had experienced fully, what they had done.

"But God meant it for good." His pit experience helped him move to the heart of the matter. Being in the pit helped him travel far, all the way to the reason for his suffering—"the saving of many lives" (Gen. 50:20). All the way to the riches of God's promises.

Pit experiences are like that. Ours certainly was. We encountered, again and again, something about God's character that lifted us, or challenged us, or chastened us.

When you encounter God in the pit, change is your only passport out.

### *The Brothers Come*

They walked into his realm
He checked his headdress
and princely garb
and stood haughty

They paid obeisance
as God told him they would.

They were hungry, he could see it—
that touched his heart.

but not enough for him
to restrain his bellowing

He hearkened back to Jacob the trickster
with mocking false accusation ("You are spies!")

The unlikely twins—love and revenge—vied for preeminence
each pulling on each other
and he was torn

He couldn't face them

But God
(just as He did with his daddy Jacob)
met him face to face
and he lived
to forgive
another day.


### Judah's Anguish (to Joseph)

Money mesmerizes my mind.
Instead of killing, I wanted to sell you.
I shame when I think of my money offer to Tamar
Shamefully I present my offering:
temporary happiness
momentary pleasure.

Again, I come in need.
Joy replaces jealousy.
But you hold the strings.

You give us food, shelter, land.
Although it is in your power to withhold,
somehow, you cannot;
and your gift is free and hilarious.

How can you forgive?
How can you use the temporal
to pursue an eternal weight of glory?

I wish I walked as weightless as you.

## A TIME FOR WAR...

### *After the Brothers Come*
*~a bitter song in the night~*

Love and hate
contend for my heart:
How can I deny my flesh?

But I want revenge
so they will taste
my bitters
without the balm

They dare to feign anguish for my father
after all the anguish they caused him!

Once, they mocked me in unbelief
Now they come to me, bowing, begging

How dare they come!

*Can you dare to forgive?*
*You must choose, Joseph.*


### *Joseph's Lament*

All my life, I have been at the mercy of others
My father's love put me at the
                    mercy of my brothers
Potiphar's wife loved me
and put me at the mercy of
my master, my jailer, Pharaoh
Even now, with my flowing robes and signet ring,
 I serve at Pharaoh's bidding
He can say the word and have my head.
I am sick of this.

Now, the tables are turned.
Judah, Simeon, all my brothers
are at my mercy.

My word can give life or death.

I will have my turn at justice.

### To Everything (Turn, Turn, Turn)

*Weep, Joseph.*
*Weep for everything*
*you know.*

I will have my turn. . .
I will have my turn. . .

Why am I weeping?
I don't want to remember
But I have to.

God, where are you taking me?
I cannot stop my weeping.
My anguish, once gnawing,
now cuts so deeply,
that I cannot stop my weeping.

They threw me mercilessly into the pit—
I can never forget the thud
as I dropped to the bottom.

I can never forget the aching hunger
for father, for family, for food,
for love.

I can never forget
how I took care of Potiphar
and he believed that woman
He had to know—didn't he?
that she was lying.

I can never forget
how the cupbearer forgot me.
I gave him such comfort.
(Didn't I save his life?)
And he never looked back
to see my suffering
and remember.

I can never forget.
I can never forget.
I can never forget.

The tears overwhelm me.
Hide them, Lord.
Let no one see them.

*I will hide them in a bottle.*
*Joseph, you can forget.*
*For I will remember you.*

### Love's Warning

*Remember, Joseph, my dear Joseph:*
*Pharaoh is my shepherd*
*as is Potiphar*
*They perform at my command*
*I have woven them into your life*

*Do not pull the threads*
*with thoughts of revenge and bitterness*
*For they will rend*
*and tear*
*the high purposes*
*of the tapestry*
*I have ordained for you.*

*Do not abuse the gift of leadership*
*For your authority*
*is vapor*
*dew on the grass*
*which the sun will burn away*
*as it grows in the sky.*

*If you cannot forgive*
*your soul*
*will grope toward wholeness*
*with fear and longing*
> *loathing*
> *even the life*
> *that I have given you.*

*I will thwart all of your ways.*
*My seraphim will keep you*
*from the tree of light and peace*
*according to your stubbornness.*
*My anger is kindled*
*because you are precious*
> *to me.*
*Behold my terror, and shrink not at My fire*
*For you will not be consumed.*

*I will withhold My favor*
*until the bending of the knee.*

*Walk around feeling like a leaf.*
*Know you could tumble any second.*
Then *decide what to do with your time.*

-*Naomi Shihab Nye*
From *The Language of Life: A Festival of Poets.* Bill Moyers, ed.

# CHAPTER EIGHT

Wings

# WINGS

Joseph came to the understanding that forgiveness is not about us, but about God (You meant it for evil, but God…). True understanding of that brought joy, and stopped the game he played with his brothers.

### *Flashback (Jacob)*

The angel smote my thigh
but only after the wrestling stretched every muscle, every fiber
The next day, the aches
kept me in my tent.

But they went away—
all except the thigh

It is a reminder
that I seen God
face to face
and lived.

His glory covers my life.

### *Flailing*

kick.

      scream.

                kick.

                    scream.

kick.

      scream.

                collapse.

Rest.

(Joseph rubs his eyes. He looks dazed.) What happened?

*You wrestled with the angel.*

What angel?

*The one reserved for hard cases.*

Was I violent?

*Quite.*

Who won?

*You both did.*

*The secret of his growing lies in this:*
*by being totally defeated and disarmed*
*by even greater forces and their cause.*

Rainer Maria Rilke. *Selected Poems.*
Translated by Albert Ernest Flemming. NY: Methuen, 1963.

## A TIME TO KEEP SILENT...

*Shhh.*

What, Lord?

*Shhh. I'm taking you to a new place today. But you have to be very quiet.*

But so many thoughts are running through my mind.

*Push them over to me. I'll hold them for you. Don't worry—you won't lose them. It is very important that you listen.*

(Joseph sits on a bench, and cocks his head.)
I hear wings beating the air. If I close my eyes tight enough, I can almost see them.

*If you relax and open them, you'll see them better.*

I see what you mean.

*You have to rest in order to really see.*

*The more times you see your way through,*
*the more comfortable you are in the dark.*

Orlando Bagwell, Producer/Director. *Eyes on the Prize*
from *I've Known Rivers: Lives of Loss and Liberation*. Sara Lawrence-Lightfoot.
Reading, MA: Addison-Wesley Pub. Co., 1994.

Three is a significant number throughout Scripture. Three is important to Joseph, too. He only forgives after the third time of weeping.

What anguish he must have felt, when he first saw his brothers standing before him. As they spoke amongst themselves, how he must have longed to do something, but what? Scream at them? Kiss them?

Joseph chose revenge after the first time of weeping, giving his brothers money to trick them. After the second weeping, his trick was even more cruel; he set up Benjamin and kept him hostage while the rest of the brothers went back to bring their father. It was only after they mentioned Jacob— and after the third weeping—that Joseph fully bent his knee to complete forgiveness.

### *Releasing & Resting*

I was in control
until they mentioned my father
and memory came
in a flood of tears

In its tide
flowed healing and forgiveness

anger fell away
I lay on the beach
peaceful

My mouth closes, but not before I say this:
My house and I
will serve the Lord

Come to me my brothers.

Reuben, first
because you tried to restrain them

Then Judah,
you who tried to walk weightless

Dan, Naphtali,
Gad, Asher, Simeon.

Levi (You are like the priests of Pharaoh)
Zebulun and Issachar

and Benjamin.

Oh, Benjamin
how I have missed you.
We came from the same womb,
and I felt your hurt across these many miles
as if it were my own.

Come, come
so that I may embrace you.

### Fight in the Heavenlies

I took a step
toward heaven today
and angered the gods
whose fires licked at my heels

they didn't know
the body they thought they were burning
was dross
that covered rock
that revealed gold.

### Jacob's Joy

I didn't think I would see you, ever
My son, all the colors of my life.
I embrace you in the flesh
Weeping wet joys.

Before, I wanted to die.
Now, I can.

I looked at the poem below some time after I wrote it, and panicked. Rachel died before Joseph's dream that his family would bow to him. He couldn't, then, have dreamed that she had bowed to him as well. It would just be too much of a stretch to make that point.

I was just about to take the entire poem out when I decided to look back at the text:

Genesis 37:10 [....and Jacob said to Joseph] shall I and thy mother and thy brethren indeed come to bow down ourselves to thee to the earth?

"Thy mother?" Joseph's mother had already died in Genesis 35:19, giving birth to Benjamin. Why would Jacob mention his beloved, departed wife?

Could it be that Jacob (and Joseph) already knew about the resurrection?

### *Reflections on a Dream*

One of my prophecies
did not come true
my mother did not bow to me
that was God's thorn

to let me know
that He
and He alone
holds knowledge
truth makes its full home only with Him
I am only a reflection:
marred humanness

How I miss my mother Rachel.

### *Reflections on a Dream, Part II*
I had a dream
my mother and father
and brothers bowed to me

My dream came true
My brothers bowed,
then wept and embraced

But my father I only embraced
He would not bow;
in my joy I would not let him.

Now it is only fitting
in the last days of his life

that I pay him homage
as he blesses my sons
and closes the circle.

### Jacob Prevails

Jacob asked for no answers.
He put away logic and explanations.
He asked, no, demanded, but one thing:
The Blessing.

### Benediction (Jacob)

The end is near
The circle closes
this time, around me

I made a vow to God
now
Joseph has made a vow to me
(I am still not able to fully trust mere promises)

Ephraim, Manasseh, come—
my strength has returned

And now
I shall span the generations
disregard convention

(as I so often have)
and bless my adopted, beloved sons.

## A TIME TO GATHER STONES TOGETHER...

### *Markings–Remembering Jacob*

Joseph (to Pharaoh)—
*I need to go back.*

Pharaoh—
*Back to where?*

Joseph—
*To the prison that finally pushed me out of its womb.*

Pharaoh—
*Why?*

Joseph—
*I want to place stones there. It is the tradition of my ancestors.
They help to mark memory, to show us what we must continue
to do.*

Pharaoh—
*How many stones will you need?*

Joseph—
*There will be 22 in all*

*One for my ancestors, Abraham and Sarah*
*who showed courage when God spoke to them*

*One for my ancestors Isaac and Rebekah*
*who followed quietly and propelled our journey forward*

*One for Esau*
*who taught my father how to forgive*

*One for my father Jacob*
*who taught me*
*both to forgive*
*and to love with abandon*

*and my mother Rachel*
*whose warmth helped me*
*to recognize the love of a woman*

*One for Potiphar*
*who trusted me*
*and prepared me to lead*

*One for you*
*an instrument of God's blessing to many*

*One each for my wife and sons*
*who helped me forget the pain of my youth*

*and one each for my brothers and my sister*
*who helped me remember*
*and then forgive*

Pharaoh—
> *What about for your God?*

Joseph—
> *My God has a Name that cannot be uttered*
> *and is a Spirit*
> *for Whom no stone will suffice*
>
> *He cannot be contained*
> *neither can He be displayed*
> *except in His creation*

# Definition

Through adversity, God introduces you to yourself.

*He has made everything beautiful in His time…*

-Ecclesiastes 3:11

### My Name is Joseph

Greetings, my brothers.
My name is Joseph.
It means "Increaser."
I didn't understand that when you put me in the pit.
I didn't know it in Potiphar's house.
I started to learn in it prison.
But now I *know*.
I know that you meant it for evil, but God meant it for good.

I understand now.

It's not about me.
It's not about my dreams, though I appreciate them.
It's about the One who gave me the interpretation.
It's not about my visions.
It's about the One who gave me sight.

I just had to know it for myself.
So I thank God for you, dear brothers.
My Father taught me, and I never forgot, I just had to learn with my heart.
I am poured out into His hands;
He is able to hold my life.

# Epilogue

*Between life and death, there is a place where one can balance the impossible.*

Amy Tan. *The Hundred Secret Senses*. NY: G.P. Putnam's Sons, 1995

### Joseph at his death
You bury me here in Egypt
but here I will not stay
before my bones turn into dust
God will make a way
for me to join my family
in the land of promise
as we journey into Promise

I am reading about the Pharaohs and it strikes me that it took great courage (nerve?) for Joseph to ask to be buried with his fathers. The Egyptian burial ritual was an apex of the culture, the final culmination of life and a way to ensure immortality. What impact must Joseph have had on his subjects when he made the request that his bones be taken from Egypt to the Promised Land, a reality that had yet to reach fruition in his time? Did

Pharaoh, friends and family think he was crazy, or that he knew something they did not know?

After all, Pharaoh did name him "Saviour of the World."

I wonder how Joseph–the–Increaser affected and impacted his Egyptian friends and loved ones. Could his wife have possibly emerged untouched by his inner and outer beauty, and by his intimate contact with a God whom she did not know? How many people, if any, changed their minds about who God was and how He worked?

I wonder if someone wrote this poem after an encounter with Joseph. It is taken from some of Egypt's oldest writings:

*I have heard the discourses of Imhotep and Hardedef with whose words men speak everywhere.*

*What are their habitations now?*

*Their walls are destroyed, their habitations are no more, as if they had never been.*

*They that build houses, their habitations are no more. What hath been done with them?*

(From *Life Under the Pharaohs*, by Leonard Cottrell.
Publisher: Holt, Rinehart & Winston , New York, 1963)

In her book, *The Same River Twice,* Alice Walker talks about being so weak and sickly at one point in her life that she could barely walk. She manages to get out of the house, and literally has to crawl on the ground to get to her destination. Her determination fascinated me, and made me think about how far we must sometimes stretch to fulfill God's purposes and tell His story.

God calls us to so much in Christ! And we are so many things—mothers and fathers, children, brothers and sisters, friends, deacons and workers in the church, employees, employers (even writers!). We must learn to go graciously back and forth, spreading riches wherever He calls us.

Peace does not reside in lying around, doing nothing. It resides in the midst of activity balanced with rest and led by the Spirit.

Joseph saw that.

### *Advice from Joseph*

Step out
and do the impossible
      interpret dreams
      have visions
juxtapose yourself:
      prisoner & caretaker
      dreamer & doer
      king and son and baby brother

as you so go
　　　back and forth
　　　your spirit will be refreshed

No matter what happens to you, you can still find comfort in doing the impossible.

*I call on Jesus*
*My life He can hold*
*I'd rather have Jesus*
*than silver and gold*

*Silver & Gold.* © *1993 Lilly Mack Music.*
*Written by Kirk Franklin. Used with permission.*

My life He can hold. My life He can hold. How I love those words.

No one knows, not even me, how many times I have said that to myself, over and over, since Terry became ill. If I did not believe that, where would I be? If I had not affirmed it to myself, listened to that song too many times to count, where would my mind be?

I shudder to think about it.

But He has held my life, and the lives of those I love, in such miraculous and surprising ways. I have learned to rejoice in those ways, and to hope in Him past all hope, and to trust when it made no sense, and to seek His face even more than I look for His blessings.

Because God glories in mystery, and the rays of His glory shine even into the secret place where I am hidden.

# Inspiration & Guidance

*And Isaac loved Esau, because he did eat of his venison: but Rebekah loved Jacob.*
Genesis 25:28 9 (KJV)

*So Rachel died and was buried on the way to Ephrath (that is, Bethlehem). Over her tomb Jacob set up a pillar, and to this day that pillar marks Rachel's tomb. Israel moved on again and pitched his tent beyond Migdal Eder.*
Genesis 35:19–21 (NIV)

*Joseph, a young man of seventeen, was tending the flocks with his brothers, the sons of Bilhah and the sons of Zilpah, his father's wives, and he brought their father a bad report about them.*
Genesis 37:1 (NIV)

*When Reuben heard this, he tried to rescue [Joseph] from their hands... "Don't shed any blood... Don't lay a hand on him."... When Reuben returned to the cistern and saw that Joseph was not there, he tore his clothes.*
Genesis 37:21-22, 29 (NIV)

*Judah said to his brothers, "Come, let's sell [Joseph] to the Ishmaelites..."*
Genesis 37:26-27 (NIV)

*And it came to pass after these things, that his master's wife cast her eyes upon Joseph; and she said, Lie with me.*
Genesis 39:7 (KJV)

*And it came to pass. . . that she called unto the men of her house, and spake unto them, saying, See, he hath brought in an Hebrew unto us to mock us; he came in unto me to lie with me, and I cried with a loud voice. . .*

*Genesis 39:14 (KJV)*

*And they replied, "We both had dreams last night; but there is no one to tell us what they mean. . . "I'll tell you what it means, Joseph told him. . . "and when you get your freedom, remember me to Pharaoh " . . .Pharaoh's cupbearer, however, promptly forgot all about Joseph. . .*

*Genesis 40:8, 18,23 (KJV)*

*And Pharaoh said unto his servants, Can we find such a one as this is, a man in whom the Spirit of God is? And Pharaoh said unto Joseph, Forasmuch as God hath shewed thee all this, there is non so discreet and wise as thou art: Thou shalt be over my house, and according unto thy word shall all my people be ruled: only in the throne will I be greater than thou. And Pharaoh said unto Joseph, See I have set thee over all the land of Egypt. . . And he made him to ride in the second chariot which he had; and they cried before him, Bow the knee: and he made him ruler over all the land of Egypt. And Pharaoh said unto Joseph, I am Pharaoh, and without thee shall no man lift up his hand or foot in all the land of Egypt. And Pharaoh called Joseph's name Zaph'nath-paaneah; and he gave him to wife Asenath the daughter of Potipherah priest of On. And Joseph went out over all the land of Egypt.*

*Genesis 41:38-41, 43-45 (KJV)*

*And he gathered up all the food of the seven years, which were in the land of Egypt, and laid up the food in the cities: the food of the field, which was round about every city, laid he up in the same. . . And all countries came into Egypt to Joseph for to buy corn; because the famine was so sore in all lands.*

*Genesis 41:48, 57 (KJV)*

*And Joseph named the first-born Manasseh, For he said, "God has made me forget all my trouble and all my father's household."*

*Genesis 41:51 (NLT)*

*And [Joseph] turned himself about from them, and wept...*

*Genesis 42:24 (KJV)*

*... they bowed down before [Joseph]...*

*Genesis 43:26 (KJV)*

*...and he sought where to weep ; and he entered into his chamber, and wept there.*
*Genesis 43:30 (KJV)*

*And he wept aloud...*

*Genesis 45:2 (KJV)*

*My son Joseph is still alive! I will go and see him before I die.*

*Genesis 45:28 (NLT)*

*"Now I am ready to die."*

*Genesis 46:30 (NIV)*

*And Israel said to Joseph, "I never expected to see your face, and now God has allowed me to see your children too."*

*Genesis 48:11-12 (NIV)*

*Then Joseph took [Ephraim and Manasseh] from his knees, and bowed with his face to the ground... And [Jacob] blessed them that day...*

*Genesis 48:12, 20a (KJV)*

*Then Joseph made the sons of Israel swear, saying, "God will surely take care of you, and you shall carry my bones away from here." So Joseph died at the age of one hundred and ten years; and he was embalmed and placed in a coffin in Egypt.*

*Genesis 50:25-26*

*Search for the Lord and His strength, and keep on searching.*

*1 Chronicles 16:11 (NLT)*

*When I am tried, I shall come forth as gold.*

*Job 23:10 (KJV)*

*For in the time of trouble, He shall hide me in His tabernacle...*

*Psalm 27:5a (KJV)*

*You have set my feet in a wide place.*

*Psalm 31:8 (Paraphrase)*

*Open your mouth wide, that I may fill it.*

*Psalm 81:10 (KJV)*

*The darkness and the light are alike to Thee.*

*Psalm 139:12 (KJV)*

*[God] says of Cyrus, He is my shepherd, and shall perform all my pleasure...*

*Isaiah 44:28 (KJV)*

*And I will give you treasures hidden in the darkness—secret riches. I will do this so you may know that I am the Lord, the God of Israel.*

*Isaiah 45:3 (NLT)*

*He was oppressed and afflicted, yet he did not open his mouth... as a sheep before her shearers is silent.*

*Isaiah 53:7-8 (NLT)*

*...to give unto them beauty for ashes ...*

*Isaiah 61:3 (KJV)*

*For I know the thoughts that I think toward you, saith the Lord, thoughts of peace, and not of evil, to give you an expected end. Then shall ye call upon me, and ye shall go and pray unto me, and I will hearken unto you. And ye shall seek me, and find me, when ye shall search for me with all you heart.*

*And I will be found of you, saith the Lord; and I will turn away your captivity...*
Jeremiah 29:11-14a (KJV)

*He reveals deep and mysterious things and knows what lies hidden in darkness, though He Himself is surrounded by light.*
Daniel 2:22 (NLT)

*I will make the Valley of Achor (trouble) a door of hope.*
Hosea 2:15

*Blessed are the poor in spirit, for theirs is the kingdom of heaven.*
Matthew 5:3 (KJV)

*For our light affliction, which is but for a moment, worketh for us a far more exceeding and eternal weight of glory.*
II Corinthians 4:17 (KJV)

*But by faith we eagerly await through the Spirit the righteousness for which we hope.*
Galatians 5:5 (KJV)

*For we are His workmanship...*
Ephesians 2:10 (KJV)

*Work out your own salvation with fear and trembling.*
Philippians 2:12 (KJV)

*For he that cometh to God must believe that He is, and that He is a rewarder of them that diligently seek Him.*

*Hebrews 11:6 (KJV)*

*By him therefore let us offer the sacrifice of praise to God continually, that is, the fruit of our lips giving thanks to his name. But to do good and communicate forget not: for with such sacrifices God is well pleased.*

*Hebrews 13:15-16 (KJV)*

For additional copies, please send $12.95
plus $1.00 shipping & handling to:

Dabar Publishing
P.O. Box 35377
Detroit, Michigan 48235